A CHRYSALIS CHILDREN'S BOOK

First published by Belitha Press in 1997
This edition first published in 2003 by
Chrysalis Children's Books, an imprint of Chrysalis Books Group plc
The Chrysalis Building, Bramley Road, London W10 6SP
www.chrysalisbooks.co.uk
Reprinted 2004 and 2005

Copyright © Chrysalis Children's Books 2003

The catalogue record for this book is available
from the British Library.

ISBN 1 84365 060 6 (mini hardback)
ISBN 1 84365 015 0 (paperback)
ISBN 1 84365 014 2 (hardback)

Printed in Singapore

4 6 8 10 9 7 5 3

This book can be ordered direct from the publisher.
Please contact the Marketing Department. But try your bookshop first.

THE
ENGLISH STRUWWELPETER
OR
PRETTY STORIES
AND
FUNNY PICTURES.

When the children have been good,
That is, be it understood,
Good at meal-times, good at play,
Good all night and good all day, —
They shall have the pretty things
Merry Christmas always brings.
Naughty, romping girls and boys
Tear their clothes and make a noise,
Spoil their pinafores and frocks,
And deserve no Christmas-box.
Such as these shall never look
At this pretty Picture-Book.

1. SHOCK-HEADED PETER.

Just look at him! There he stands,
With his nasty hair and hands.
See! his nails are never cut;
They are grim'd as black as soot;
And the sloven, I declare,
Never once has comb'd his hair;
Any thing to me is sweeter
Than to see Shock-headed Peter.

2. THE STORY OF CRUEL FREDERICK.

Here is cruel Frederick, see!
A horrid wicked boy was he;
He caught the flies, poor little things,
And then tore off their tiny wings,
He kill'd the birds, and broke the chairs,
And threw the kitten down the stairs;
And Oh! far worse than all beside,
He whipp'd his Mary, till she cried.

The trough was full, and faithful Tray
Came out to drink one sultry day;
He wagg'd his tail, and wet his lip,
When cruel Fred snatch'd up a whip,
And whipp'd poor Tray till he was sore,
And kick'd and whipp'd him more and more:
At this, good Tray grew very red,
And growl'd and bit him till he bled;
Then you should only have been by,
To see how Fred did scream and cry!

So Frederick had to go to bed;
His leg was very sore and red!
The Doctor came and shook his head,
And made a very great to-do,
And gave him nasty physic too.

But good dog Tray is happy now;
He has no time to say "bow-wow!"
He seats himself in Frederick's chair
And laughs to see the nice things there:
The soup he swallows, sup by sup, —
And eats the pies and puddings up.

3. THE DREADFUL STORY ABOUT HARRIET AND THE MATCHES.

It almost makes me cry to tell
What foolish Harriet befell.
Mamma and Nurse went out one day
And left her all alone at play;
Now, on the table close at hand,
A box of matches chanc'd to stand;
And kind Mamma and Nurse had told her,
That, if she touch'd them, they should scold her.
But Harried said: "O, what a pity!
For, when they burn, it is so pretty;
They crackle so, and spit, and flame;
Mamma, too, often does the same."

The pussy-cats heard this,
And they began to hiss,
And stretch their claws
And raise their paws;
"Me-ow," they said, "me-ow, me-o,
You'll burn to death, if you do so."

But Harriet would not take advice,
She lit a match, it was so nice!
It crackled so, it burn'd so clear, —
Exactly like the picture here.
She jump'd for joy and ran about
And was too pleas'd to put it out.

The pussy-cats saw this
And said: "Oh, naughty, naughty Miss!"
And stretch'd their claws
And rais'd their paws:
"'Tis very, very wrong, you know,
Me-ow, me-o, me-ow, me-o,
You will be burnt, if you do so".

And see! Oh! what a dreadful thing!
The fire has caught her apron-string;
Her apron burns, her arms, her hair;
She burns all over, everywhere.

Then how the pussy-cats did mew,
What else, poor pussies, could they do?
They scream'd for help, 'twas all in vain!
So then, they said: "we'll scream again;
Make haste, make haste, me-ow, me-o,
She'll burn to death, we told her so."

So she was burnt, with all her clothes,
And arms, and hands, and eyes, and nose;
Till she had nothing more to lose
Except her little scarlet shoes;
And nothing else but these was found
Among her ashes on the ground.

And when the good cats sat beside
The smoking ashes, how they cried!
"Me-ow, me-oo, me-ow, me-oo,
What will Mamma and Nursy do?"
Their tears ran down their cheeks so fast;
They made a little pond at last.

4. THE STORY OF THE INKY BOYS.

As he had often done before,
The woolly-headed black-a-moor
One nice fine summer's day went out
To see the shops and walk about;
And as he found it hot, poor fellow,
He took with him his green umbrella.
Then Edward, little noisy wag,
Ran out and laugh'd, and wav'd his flag;
And William came in jacket trim
And brought his wooden hoop with him;
And Arthur. too, snatch'd up his toys
And join'd the other naughty boys;
So, one and all set up a roar
And laugh'd and hooted more and more,
And kept on singing, — only think! —
"Oh! Blacky, you're as black as ink."

Now tall Agrippa lived close by, —
So tall, he almost touch'd the sky;
He had a mighty inkstand too,
In which a great goose-feather grew;
He call'd out in an angry tone:
"Boys, leave the black-a-moor alone!
For if he tries with all his might,
He cannot change from black to white."
But ah! they did not mind a bit
What great Agrippa said of it;
But went on laughing, as before,
And hooting at the black-a-moor.

Then great Agrippa foams with rage,
Look at him on this very page!
He seizes Arthur, seizes Ned,
Takes William by his little head;

And they may scream and kick and call.
Into the ink he dips them all;
Into the inkstand, one, two, three,
Till they are black, as black can be;
Turn over now and you shall see.

See, there they are, and there they run!
The black-a-moor enjoys the fun.
They have been made as black as crows,
Quite black all over, eyes and nose,
And legs, and arms, and heads, and toes,
And trowsers, pinafores, and toys, —
Tho' silly little inky boys!
Because they set up such a roar,
And teas'd the harmless black-a-moor.

5. THE STORY OF THE MAN THAT WENT OUT SHOOTING.

This is the man that shoots the hares;
This is the coat he always wears:
With game-bag, powder-horn and gun
He's going out to have some fun.

The hare sits snug in leaves and grass,
And laughs to see the green man pass.

He finds it hard, without a pair
Of spectacles, to shoot the hare.

Now, as the sun grew very hot,
And he a heavy gun had got,
He lay down underneath a tree
And went to sleep, as you may see.
And, while he slept like any top,
The little hare came, hop, hop, hop,
Took gun and spectacles, and then
On her hind legs went off again.

The green man wakes and sees her place
The spectacles upon her face;
And now she's trying all she can,
To shoot the sleepy, green-coat man.
He cries and screams and runs away;
The hare runs after him all day
And hears him call out everywhere:
"Help! Fire! Help! The Hare! The Hare!"

At last he stumbled at the well
Head over ears, and in he fell.
The hare stopp'd short, took aim, and hark!
Bang went the gun, — she miss'd her mark!

The poor man's wife was drinking up
Her coffee in her coffee-cup;
The gun shot cup and saucer through;
"O dear!" cried she, "what shall I do?"
There liv'd close by the cottage there
The hare's own child, the little hare;
And while she stood upon her toes,
The coffee fell and burn'd her nose.
"O dear!" she cried, with spoon in hand,
"Such fun I do not understand."

6. THE STORY OF LITTLE SUCK-A-THUMB.

One day, Mamma said: "Conrad dear.
I must go out and leave you here.
But mind now, Conrad, what I say,
Don't suck your thumb while I'm away.
The great tall tailor always comes
To little boys that suck their thumbs,
And ere they dream what he's about,
He takes his great sharp scissors out
And cuts their thumbs clean off, — and then,
You know, they never grow again."

Mamma had scarcely turn'd her back,
The thumb was in, Alack! Alack!

The door flew open, in he ran,
The great, long, red-legg'd scissor-man.
Oh! children, see! the tailor's come
And caught out little Suck-a-Thumb.
Snip! Snap! Snip! the scissors go;
And Conrad cries out — Oh! Oh! Oh!
Snip! Snap! Snip! They go so fast,
That both his thumbs are off at last.

Mamma comes home; there Conrad stands.
And looks quite sad, and shows his hands, —
"Ah!" said Mamma "I knew he'd come
To naughty little Suck-a-Thumb."

(16)

7. THE STORY OF AUGUSTUS WHO WOULD NOT HAVE ANY SOUP.

Augustus was a chubby lad;
Fat ruddy cheeks Augustus had;
And every body saw with joy
The plump and hearty healthy boy.
He ate and drank as he was told,
And never let his soup get cold.
But one day, one cold winter's day,
He scream'd out — "Take the soup away!
O take the nasty soup away!
I won't have any soup to-day."

Next day, now look, the picture shows
How lank and lean Augustus grows!
Yet, though he feels so weak and ill,
The naughty fellow cries out still —
"Not any soup for me, I say:
O take the nasty soup away;
I won't have any soup to-day."

The third day comes; Oh what a sin!
To make himself so pale and thin.
Yet, when the soup is put on table,
He screams, as loud as he is able, —
"Not any soup for me. I say:
O take the nasty soup away!
I won't have any soup to-day."

Look at him, now the fourth day's come!
He scarcely weighs a sugar-plum;
He's like a little bit of thread,
And on the fifth day, he was — dead!

8. THE STORY OF FIDGETY PHILIP.

Let me see if Philip can
Be a little gentleman;
Let me see, if he is able
To sit still for once at table:
Thus Papa bade Phil behave;
And Mamma look'd very grave.
But fidgety Phil,
He won't sit still;
He wriggles
And giggles,
And then, I declare,
Swings backwards and forwards
And tilts up his chair,
Just like any rocking horse; —
"Philip! I am getting cross!"

See the naughty restless child
Growing still more rude and wild.
Till his chair falls over quite.
Philip screams with all his might.
Catches at the cloth, but then
That makes matters worse again.
Down upon the ground they fall.
Glasses, plates, knives, forks and all.
How Mamma did fret and frown.
When she saw them tumbling down!
And Papa made such a face!
Philip is in sad disgrace.

Where is Philip, where is he?
Fairly cover'd up you see!
Cloth and all are lying on him;
He has pull'd down all upon him.
What a terrible to-do!
Dishes, glasses, snapt in two!
Here a knife, and there a fork!
Philip, this is cruel work.
Table all so bare, and ah!
Poor Papa, and poor Mamma
Look quite cross, and wonder how
They shall make their dinner now.

9. THE STORY OF JOHNNY HEAD-IN-AIR.

As he trudg'd along to school,
It was always Johnny's-rule
To be looking at the sky
And the clouds that floated by;
But what just before him lay,
In his way,
Johnny never thought about;
So that every one cried out —
"Look at little Johnny there,
Little Johnny Head-In-Air!"

Running just in Johnny's way,
Came a little dog one day;
Johnny's eyes were still astray
Up on high,
In the sky;
And he never heard them cry —
"Johnny, mind, the dog is nigh!"
Bump!
Dump!
Down they fell, with such a thump,
Dog and Johnny in a lump!

Once, with head as high as ever,
Johnny walk'd beside the river.
Johnny watch'd the swallows trying
Which was cleverest at flying.
Oh! what fun!
Johnny watch'd the bright round sun
Going in and coming out;
This was all he thought about.
So he strode on, only think!
To the river's very brink,
Where the bank was high and steep,
And the water very deep;
And the fishes, in a row,
Stared to see him coming so.

One step more! Oh! sad to tell!
Headlong in poor Johnny fell.
And the fishes, in dismay,
Wagg'd their tails and ran away.

There lay Johnny on his face,
With his nice red writing-case;
But, as they were passing by,
Two strong men had heard him cry;
And, with sticks, these two strong men
Hook'd poor Johnny out again.

Oh! you should have seen him shiver
When they pull'd him from the river
He was in a sorry plight!
Dripping wet, and such a fright!
Wet all over, everywhere,
Clothes, and arms, and face, and hair
Johnny never will forget
What it is to be so wet.

And the fishes, one, two, three,
Are come back again, you see;
Up they came the moment after,
To enjoy the fun and laughter.
Each popp'd out his little head.
And, to tease poor Johnny, said:
"Silly little Johnny, look,
You have lost your writing-book!"

10. THE STORY OF FLYING ROBERT.

When the rain comes tumbling down
In the country or the town,
All good little girls and boys
Stay at home and mind their toys.
Robert thought, — "No, when it pours,
It is better out of doors."
Rain it d i d, and in a minute
Bob was in it.
Here you see him, silly fellow,
Underneath his red umbrella.

What a wind! Oh! how it whistles
Through the trees and flow'rs and thistles!
It has caught his red umbrella;
Now look at him, silly fellow,
Up he flies
To the skies.
No one heard his screams and cries,
Through the clouds the rude wind bore him,
And his hat flew on before him.

Soon they got to such a height,
They were nearly out of sight!
And the hat went up so high,
That it really touch'd the sky
No one ever yet could tell
Where they stopp'd, or where they fell:
Only, this one thing is plain,
Bob was never seen again!

——————

Printed in Singapore